THE FIFTH HORSEMAN

To: thedevil@hell.hel

From: tjwormwood@7circle.com

Re: Destroying the Global Economy, and other issues

(As hacked by Bill Blain)

CONTENTS

ABOUT THIS POLEMIC

Bill Blain is an investment banker and strategist, market commentator and broadcaster on Financial matters. Bill's daily "*Morning Porridge*" Blog and Weekly Podcast "*The Financial Porridge*" are distributed across the financial markets. His audience and clients include senior Central Bankers, Regulators and a smattering of Politicians – all of whom might be peeved at this Polemic - which suggests bad decisions might just be responsible for the miserable state of the Global Economy.

If you were thinking you've bought an exciting romance involing occult finance and a heroic demonic banker - sorry, my bad!

You have bought a short book, a Polemic, about how destructive the last 10-years of bad decisions by politicians, bankers, central bankers and politicians have been for all of us. Since none of the people at fault are likely to listen, and very few folk outside finance are likely to care, Bill thought he may as well make a joke out of it... because there is nothing funnier than a really good laugh at ourselves..

So.... let us begin...

A few weeks ago, after a particularly good night out, Bill dreamt there was a sudden bright shining light in the bedroom, the muted sound of a celestial choir, and a flapping of wings. He woke up with a harp still ringing in his ears to find a memory stick on his pillow with the following email chains and attachments recorded on it.

The emails are fascinating - outlining a demonic plan to subvert and destroy the global economy.

Oh, Gosh! How unlikely is that....

In a series of emails between Hell's top banker and his boss, the devil and the demon discuss exactly how they destroyed global prosperity, increased income inequality, did Brexit, got Donald Trump elected, and what they intend to do next to really ruin our day, our tomorrow, the day after that and everything else...

To avoid the courts, the characters in this Polemic are in no way related to or based on anyone alive, dead or ever worked for Goldman Sachs.

Bill Blain

July 2019

CHAIN 1

AN IDEA FOR YOUR CONSIDERATION - THE FIFTH HORSEMAN?

From: TJ Wormwood, L3R7C <tjwormwood@7circle.com>
To: Lucifer, Lord of Infinite Darkness <thedevil@hel.hel>
Subject: A new idea for your consideration? The Fifth Horseman

Dear L'LOID

Thanks for the bonus on the successful delivery of the first stage of the China vs US project! (I will use the defrocked bishops to build an organ – pricking 'em with sharp pointy sticks to make them squeal and squeak in dis-harmony.) I really do think this China vs America trade war is going to end very badly for everyone concerned with all kinds of unintended consequences – It's going to be a screaming success!

It's amazing how the old wiles always work the best. There is nothing as simple as whispering into the ears of a few key players some variation on the old theme of "a great empire will be destroyed if you invade now". The fools in Washington have absolutely no idea who... Offer mankind an apple, and they will devour it!

Following the last board meeting in the California Redwood Glade you challenged us to find new ways to destabilise human society and increase the general sum of misery.

I have an idea...

I think we're underestimating the potential presented by Global Financial Markets. I never expected the GFC, the "Global Financial Crisis", I engineered in 2007 would still be so dominant and destabilising 12 years later. The consequences and flawed policy responses have been phenomenal: low growth, youth unemployment, rising income inequality and political instability. We are now unravelling the era of Free Trade, economic liberalism and globalisation, clearly we've been painting all these broadly positive economic forces as inherently bad. We've made every country suspicious of each other's foreign exchange policy and put currency manipulation at the core of disputes! The potential for further disruption is greater than we ever anticipated.

I've spent my whole career since *The Fall* in your service driving greed and avarice. Without blowing my own celestial trumpet, I've invented and committed every single financial crime from Usury, Paper Money, Derivatives and Insider Trading. I collapsed the Roman Empire by debasing the coinage, bankrupted Scotland through the Darien Scheme (and nearly repeated it in England with the South Sea Bubble), facilitated World War II through hyper-inflation in Germany, and crafted all the great market crashes of the last 100 years. I've whispered into the ears of the all the great fraudsters and financial idiots from Nero, Louis XIV and John Law, Madoff, and nearly every single current central banker – some are more receptive than others.

But nothing in my entire experience has worked quiet so well as the GFC I began in 2007.

I've tried to figure out why it's been so successful. I've concluded there is almost unlimited potential to use Modern Financial Markets to utterly confound, confuse and befuddle mankind. The possibilities to guide them into the wrong choices are limitless. Encouraging markets to mimic mankind's greed, sloth, ignorance, price and avarice, while giving them a few nods in the wrong direction, means they are blinded to the consequences of their actions.

We must be careful. Although the GFC dramatically has held back growth and crushed the hopes and expectations of many over the last decade, its' equally clear financial markets have historically been a tremendous force for good. The "rational" and efficient allocation of resources and ease of exchange has created wealth, prosperity, raised global living standards, health, education and social cohesion. I am increasingly convinced Financial Markets were pioneered and innovated by the **Other Side**, and suspect **Hemself** has been feeding ideas and concepts to financial thinkers **Shi** has been nurturing.

Continuing the destabilisation of Financial Markets offer 2 opportunities:

Firstly, we can use them to amplify and encourage sin: greed, gluttony, avarice and all the other human behaviours. In the right hands, and properly manipulated, we are positive Financial Markets will prove the ultimate weapon for mankind to author their own destruction.

Secondly, by demonising financial markets we will be dramatically diminishing their effectiveness for the future improvement of the human condition and striking direct at **Hemself's** Divine Plan. If we make mankind believe its financial markets to blame, rather than their own behaviours, then we diminish the opportunities they create for improving their lot.

I therefore propose a new **Fifth Horseman** to add to the Four: "**Financial Meltdown**".

I'm thinking of the character from the Monopoly Game riding a particularly Fat Horse? It will be a simple metaphor to keep ongoing financial collapse disturbing and fresh in the global mindset.

As a Very Senior Banker advising governments, central banks, supranational organisations, hedge funds and the world's largest corporations I should be able to throw suggestions and plant a few seeds to direct and influence global markers in whatever direction we choose.

If we can undo the effectiveness of markets in improving the human lot, the **Other Side** and **Hemself** is going to go ballistic when *shi* finds out what we've done!

Regards
Thaddeus J. Wormwood

Lord of the 3rd Ring of the 7th Circle,
Chief Demonic Officer – Finance

From: thedevil@hell.com

To: tjwormwood@7circle.com

Subject: Re: A new Idea for your consideration? The Fifth Horseman

TJ

Great to hear from you.

Fifth Horseman sounds interesting. It has a certain "ring" to it. Not sure monopoly man on a porky horse achieves the effect you are looking for...

Heard you gave a good spiel at Davos on the same theme. Send me a copy.

Speak later.

NICK

From: TJ Wormwood, L3R7C

To: Lucifer, Lord of Infinite Darkness:

Subject: Re: Re: A new idea for your consideration? The Fifth Horseman

Attachment – WordFile – Davos Jan 19

Dear L'LIOD

Very pleased to hear you got good reports from Davos. Shame you weren't there. Please find a copy attached of my opening comments at DAVOS where I touched on some of the themes I've been thinking about re The Fifth Horseman concept. I think it's also on YouDarkTube?

I must say, the Chinese representatives have some very interesting angles to consider, and the funny little fellow from Korea is hilarious.

Warmest Regards

TJ

From: thedevil@hell.hel

To: tjwormwood@7circle.com

Subject: Re: Re: Re A new idea for your consideration? The Fifth Horseman

TJ

I dropped into Davos but had a scheduling conflict with one the social media firms we own. Even I can't be two places at once.

I can't open the file?

Can I open Word with my Mac-Book?

NICK

CHAIN 2:

Wormwood's Comments at Davos – Jan 2019

ATTACHMENT – DOWNLOADED - FILE: Wormwood Comments at Davos – Jan 2019

(Edited version of the speech given by the TJ Wormwood, Lord of 3rd Ring of the 7th Circle, to invited audience at Davos.)

Dear Colleagues,

As you all know, I've been wrecking finance for millennia. [**Pause for effect**]

Nearly every major big idea, evolutionary leap forward, invention and discovery has improved the miserable lot of mankind only through their ability to monetise it. Forget the theft of fire – being able to monetise fire by attracting pretty and willing mates around a warm campfire, or cooking the food others have hunted, is what mattered. Strip out the noise, and the rise of mankind is largely due to improvements in the efficiency and ease of means of exchange.

*From the realisation hunters could barter their furs for other goods, to the rise of complex products to finance global growth – the innovation of financial markets has been a major driver of success for the **Other Side** in raising the wellbeing and prosperity of mankind. Pretty much anything that holds back or disrupts trade, increases costs and holds back services is naturally positive for our goal of global destabilisation.*

So, here is the big plan:

*We are going to turn the **Other Side's** successful innovation of financial markets against them. Global Financial Markets are incredibly rich in opportunities to distort truth, hide lies, and undermine mankind – generating immediate greed, envy, suspicion and anger. We've uncovered previously unimaginable ways in which to financially* *screw the World with consequences that impact everyone.*

We've overlaid the programme with our mastery and understanding of temptation, human greed, avarice and pride, while adding subtlety and cunning. We merely suggest and advise. We are facilitating the train-wreck of the global economy by destroying asset values while confounding their understanding of money and wealth – the pillars of their society.

At its simplest form we are manipulating and driving constant market instability to keep mankind distracted. Uncertainty clouds their future expectations – so we keep it raining. A Mortgage crisis one year, followed by a Sovereign Debt crisis the next, spiced with a couple of bank failures, and threats of global trade war. Overlay with confusion and distraction such as social media, fake news, Bitcoin and populism, and it all works rather well.

Keep their leaders arguing. Keep the blame game going.

Our success can be seen in current financial asset prices. These are now hopelessly inflated and distorted by foolish post financial crisis policy decisions. They are bubbles set to pop. Empower the regulators and bureaucrats to compromise finance through zealous over-regulation, making banking safer by destroying it. Usher in a new era of trade protectionism, the end of Free Trade and increase the suspicion some countries are manipulating their currencies for economic advantage. Sprinkle some dust of political catastrophe, the collapse of law, undo the fair, just and caring society, while adding some eye of newt and complex environmental threats. Make the rich so rich they don't notice, and the poor so poor they become invisible. If the markets remain uncertain, then it distracts mankind from addressing these issues, making society less stable!

There as some things we're really proud of, including the Euro, Social Media, Investment Banks, the Tech Boom, and especially Quantitative Easing (which is still delivering confusion and pain).

New Monetary Theory could prove even better – it shows tremendous potential to thoroughly unsettle confidence in money. Cybercurrencies are particularly fun – despite coming up with the idea, neither we, nor even the distinguished members of our panel of eternal guests, understand the why of them. The are libertarian nonsense – so, naturally we continue to encourage them as get-rich-quick schemes, but they also further undermine confidence in money and government. We made something up in a bar one night and called it a Distributed Ledger - the humans ran with it and invented Blockchain, whatever that might be..

Some of the other stuff we've encouraged, such as The EU, ETFs, Hi-Frequency Trading, Neil Woodford and Deutsche Bank look likely to be highly effective vectors of short-term economic destruction and de-stabilisation, triggering systemic market events and regulatory backlashes across markets. We are only now exploring the full potential of market illiquidity to rob billions of pensioners of their savings.

We've persuaded investors to overturn proven tried and tested investment strategies and wisdoms, nurturing a whole range of overpriced unprofitable US Tech "Unicorn" companies which we are confident will prove utterly over-hyped and largely worthless. The success of social media, data mining and new tech has increased levels of dissatisfaction and envy – especially in our target younger demography.

The way we successfully pinned the blame on banks for the Global Financial Crisis – despite the fact it was people who wanted mortgages to buy houses and fast cars - ensured global regulators would over-react. We've allowed regulators to focus on banks while we target the next financial crisis in other parts of the financial ecosystem.

Regulators forced the banks to de-risk. But risk does not disappear - it just goes somewhere else. While banks understood risk and had massive staffs to manage risk, risk is now concentrated in the hands of "investment managers" who are singularly ill-equipped to withstand the next credit crunch and global recession, (which we've planned for next October – Save the Date cards have been sent).

We are particularly pleased that many banks now exceed the 2.3 compliance officers for every profitable banker ratio. Compliance and regulatory costs now exceed 10% of income at some European banks – a stunning success and substantially decreasing the efficiency of banking and exchanges.

We've some great new financial ideas we are still experimenting with, some of which show great promise for further weakening society. Facebook Money is going to be a cracker, and I particularly like the Spaceship to Mars project... if only they knew what awaits them...

By hiding inflation in the stock market, we assisted the accumulation of massive wealth by a tiny percentage of the population to ferment income inequality dissatisfaction. When capital is concentrated and the workers under the cosh, it creates all the right conditions for weak disjointed government to aid and abet the rise of destabilising populism.

It's highly satisfying to watch the instability we've created in financial markets drive fear and distrust across society. The debt crisis we engineered led to global financial austerity, job insecurity, and rising inequality. We were surprised how easily we pushed the Gig economy concept to further exploit and cow workers through regulators and authorities – they barely noticed. Over this we've layered whole new levels of anxiety such as the unknowns of data theft, the rise in envy coefficients through social media, fake news while fuelling social distrust through resentment.

We've managed to persuade Governments to follow damaging and contradictory policies. As society reeled in the wake of the financial crisis, we persuaded policy makers to cut back spending through "austerity" spending programmes, simultaneously bailing out bankers while flooding the financial economy with free money through Quantitative Easing.

Effectively we've split the world into two economies. A real economy which is sad, miserable and deflating, and a financial economy that's insanely optimistic, massively inflated and ripe to pop on the back of free money.

The resentment, instability, fear and general sense of decay has paid dividends in our drive to break society by undermining the credibility of the political classes. Our approach to politics has been simple – deskill the political classes, reduce their effectiveness as leaders, while engineering economic, social and financial instability to drive rampaging populist politics – just like in 1932! Populism may ultimately prove short-lived, but it's difficult to see how the political classes will recover their power in time to reverse the damages being done to the global environment.

While markets have burned, society become increasingly riven, and politics has failed, we've distracted the humans from the rising levels of carbon dioxide in the atmosphere which threatens to create global warming and rising sea levels, while plastics poison the oceans and soil erosion threatens agriculture.

Now I love the ravenous hunger and sharp pointy teeth of polar bears as much as the next demon, but needs must... needs must. I was also rather fond of the dinosaurs...

Our approach to ensuring destructive climate change has proved very effective. We've supported, financed and advised the loudest green lobbies to ensure their message looks ill-considered, wrong and economic suicide. We also paid big bucks to fund the loudest climate change deniers. Our innovation of fake news to discredit and mitigate anything positive means climate change remains a crank topic – even as our polar bears drown.

Meanwhile, through our dominance of global boardrooms and investment firms, we've made sure that large corporates have bought-out and stifled new technologies that could solve the environmental crisis.

Our future looks great – because their future is bleak!

Thank you for your kind attention.

TJ Wormwood,
Demonic Chief Office
Lord 3rd Ring, 7th Circle

From: TJ Wormwood, L3R7C

To: Lucifer, Lord of Infinite Darkness:

Subject: Davos and Project Fifth Horseman

Dear B'LOID

Hope you found my speech to the Davos crowd interesting? Any comment? I would be very interested in your thoughts?

Can I roll with the Fifth Horseman project?

Warm Regards

TJ Wormwood

L3R7C

From: thedevil@hell.hel

To: tjwormwood@7circle.com

Subject: Re: Davos and Project Fifth Horseman

TJ, Tx.

Will get back to you. I have some concerns I want to think through...

What's the Orange guy up to re Mexico? Keep him focused on Europe and China!

NICK

CHAIN 3:

Fifth Horseman Project Proposal, Rules and Parameters

From: thedevil@hell.hel

To: tjwormwood@7circle.com

Subject: Re: Fifth Horseman – Project Proposal, Rules and Parameters

TJ

Read your speech. Very good. After due consideration, run with Fifth Horseman project.

But there are hoops to go through...

It will need to go through the Demonic Advisory Board (DAB). As you would expect, they are bunch of complete bastards.

There is stuff I still need to think about. I don't want to alert *hem* up there with a formal rewrite and reprint of the Biblical Apocalypse stuff. That will create some employment and title issues around the new Fifth Horseman position if it isn't formalised in same way as the other four. We can deal with that later...

I need a short, sharp Teaser note to get the DAB excited. It will also need a "Mission Statement", and all the other crap these guys demand. If you get the Teaser right, it should drive itself.

You also need to put the plan through Compliance, Legal and HR to make sure you don't breach the Constantinople Rules. We don't want to upset *Hemself* and *Hir* Combined Divine Hosts. Let me remind you of the critical rules:

i)   You can't play the full suite of Apocalypse Cards together.

That would be construed as "END OF DAYS". Who wants that…? Messy! But a small war here, a famine there, and a plague way over there is fine. Playing the whole suite of cards together and sending them trampling over everything tends to rather undo the fun of suborning the good and spreading evil.

ii) You can only suggest but may not direct ideas and concepts. (I'm sure you are aware there are ways round this.)

iii) You need to clearly show whatever mayhem is achieved, they do it to themselves and blame themselves.

**Regards
NICK**

From: TJ Wormwood, L3R7C

To: Lucifer, Lord of Infinite Darkness:

Subject: Re: Fifth Horseman – Project Proposal, Rules and Parameters

L'LOID

How about this for a Mission Statement?

Project Fifth Horseman aims to Engineer on-going financial disaster, distortion, uncertainty and distraction by utilising Global Financial Markets to make the world a much less pleasant place"

Snappy enough?

TJ

From: thedevil@hell.hel

To: tjwormwood@7circle.com

Subject: Re: Re: Fifth Horseman – Project Proposal, Rules and Parameters

That works.

Nick

CHAIN 4:

The Teaser and 10,000 Foot View

From: TJ Wormwood, L3R7C

To: Lucifer, Lord of Infinite Darkness:

Subject: Fifth Horseman Teaser

L'LOID

How about the following for the **Teaser**? It's the 10,000 feet perspective. A top down explanation. It's got nice clear bullet points so even the thickest of your host of minions can quickly grasp the potential.

I think it captures the opportunity. If you agree, I'll then draw up a short briefing note looking at the 4 main strategies we suggest using in the campaign to follow it up.

Regards

TJ

(L3R7C)

FILE DOWNLOAD - PROJECT FIFTH HORSEMAN TEASER

GLOBAL FINANCIAL MELTDOWN – The Fifth Horseman

Our use of global financial markets to ferment the ongoing Global Financial Crisis that began in 2007 has succeeded beyond our wildest hopes. We have broken market confidence, successfully undermined global political processes, spawned untold damage to global economic growth - crushed the hopes and aspirations of billions - and yet again proved mankind has little understanding of the universal laws of unintended consequences.

The negative benefits to mankind directly attributable to the financial crisis include:

- Reversed Global Growth
- Lower Positive Aspirations
- Reduced the Credibility of both Democratic and State Control political systems
- Ended Free Trade and replaced it with Protectionism
- Increased suspicions between people and peoples
- Enslaved workers through the GIG economy, student and personal debt
- Divided Society and Rendered Social Cohesion
- Raised Geopolitical Tensions
- Undone improvements in Health, Education and Welfare
- Stamped out the rule of Law
- Widened Inequality
- Destroyed the Environment

These are all laudable goals!

The next stage will be to launch new initiatives to further deepen trade protectionism, the end of globalisation, and engineering the collapse of confidence in global fiat money - which will cause nations to tumble into even steeper decline and back toward barter economies. All these factors will distract them from the environmental degradation that will soon make much of the planet uninhabitable.

Through our proxies we have successfully manipulated markets and destabilised society. We've pinned the blame for increasing uncertainty and decreasing happiness on capitalism and governments. We've created a fertile bed of resentment, envy and anger into which we may plant the seeds of further social unrest and destabilisation. Global growth is reversing, the environment deteriorating, and incomes are tumbling for all but the richest 0.01%.

Society is riven. Hope is dying as the young realise they face lives of hopeless wage slavery trying to keep their heads above debt. We have compromised the health, judicial, and social welfare networks that once threatened to improve the quality of life and create fairer and equal societies.

The rich Western nations of the world are slowing and contracting, the US and Europe are diverging and increasingly distrustful of each other. The emerging nations of Asia are coalescing round China and India and demanding more of a declining economic pie. The prospects for global conflict haven't looked this favourable and likely for years. The prospects for an all-out China vs US shooting war brought on by trade wars, currency manipulation and geopolitics are most promising. We're planning to deal with China as soon as finish with the Yanks... Europe is taking care of itself!

The plan is complex, multi-layered, and it's working rather well.

We now propose to up the pressure by introducing a new Fifth Horseman – *"Financial Meltdown".* This will prove a figure to rally the increasing doubts mankind has about global markets around. Building social expectations of imminent financial catastrophe will cloud and strain sentiment and dent hope of global recovery – keeping misery quotients at elevated levels.

We believe *Hemself*'s own financial advisors have been driving global markets as a force for good. It's time we show them to have been utterly wrong!

TJ Wormwood,

CDO Fifth Horseman Project

L3R7C

CHAIN 5:

The Mechanics of Market De-struction – made simple

From: TJ Wormwood, L3R7C

To: Lucifer, Lord of Infinite Darkness:

Subject: THE MECHANICS OF MARKET DESTRUCTION – made simple

Attachment – WordFile: Strategy Paper on Project Fifth Horseman

L'LOID

Please find attached the paper you requested outlining the mechanics of the Fifth Horseman proposal.

Regards

TJ

L3R7C

FILE DOWNLOAD – Mechanics v2

The Mechanics of Market Destruction: QE, Regulation, Austerity and Politics

Following the nadir of the Global Financial Crisis in 2008, stock markets have risen over 200%. Other financial asset classes have posted similar stellar gains. Investors have done exceedingly well. Yet, the sum of human happiness has dramatically diminished. Human wealth has not increased – stocks and shares are higher, but real assets have barely changed. While the authorities worry about deflation in the real world, inflation is hidden in financial assets.

We've achieved stunning success by playing a classic distraction con – focus the mark on what the left hand is doing, while the right hand robs them blind.

Presidents, bankers and fund managers congratulate themselves on the success of the economy in terms of the gains in stock prices, their booming personal wealth, and how much patronising philanthropy they undertake.

The simple truth is workers are paid less today in real terms than they were pre-crisis. As the gig-economy takes hold, workers find themselves with less security, less welfare provision, their salaries buying less while local services deteriorate, abandoned and aren't replaced. Real earnings have tumbled, while the bulk of their taxes now go to paying grossly inflated civil service pensions.

Western economies are in worse shape with decaying infrastructure and obsolete factories. Health services can barely cope with the ravages of old-age, obesity caused by unhealthy eating, rising drug abuse, and diminished funding. Educational standards are dropping as students are forced to enter indentured servitude to finance their sub-optimal courses. Little thought is given to the future needs of modern economies as politicians are distracted by irrelevancies including Brexit.

The problems of the developing world are getting substantially worse and more difficult to address as we keep the rich nations focused on their own deepening problems. Human misery is increasing across the globe.

All these things can be fixed. It is our objective to ensure they are not, by keeping mankind distracted, unbalanced, uncertain, and never stop them making mistakes.

It's useful to understand the four major forces we've utilised to wreck the global economy. We are utilising four main strategies:

1) Quantitative Easing, Monetary Experimentation and Modern Monetary Theory

QE has proved one of our most effective methods for creating long-term financial instability by creating unsustainable distortion. In the face of what our operatives in the media and financial analysis described as the *"imminent meltdown of the global economy"*, we encouraged Central Bankers to embrace a magical money tree theory of monetary experimentation on an unprecedented grand scale. We warned them inflation would be a consequence but didn't tell them where to look for it. An immediate global recession was avoided, but the unforeseen and unintended consequences have been remarkable and will proved long lived.

QE effects include:

- *Forced investors to take greater risks and invest in less liquid markets*
- *Hid inflation in Financial Assets – causing massive pricing distortions across all asset classes.*
- *Split the deflationary real economy from the inflationary financial economy*
- *Driven a debt fuelled corporate borrowing binge and fuelled Corporate stock buybacks,*
- *Accelerated income inequality*
- *Stalled business investment and innovation*

Our latest wheeze is Modern Monetary Theory, a heavy free-spending variation on Keynesian economics we've concocted and encouraged as essentially free unlimited cold-fusion money. It could be even more destructive than QE with the added advantages of:

- *Transferring inflation back into the real economy.*
- *Diminishing confidence in Global Fiat Money*
- *Putting Governments into the economic driving seat, enhancing the power of bureaucracy and inefficiency.*

2) Regulatory Overkill

Regulators and bureaucrats failed to spot and act on the causes ahead of the GFC in 2007/08, missing the potential threats posed by the proliferation of "instruments of financial destruction" such as swaps, derivatives, CLOs, CDOs, and securitisation. They failed to act on the build up of lax underwriting standards across mortgage and other borrowing markets. They failed to anticipate what would happen if global monetary flows were shut-off and failed to provide liquidity when they did.

The global regulatory community didn't understand how markets worked then – addressing the symptoms of the crisis in terms of inappropriate debt instruments and failed banking, rather than the causes: heavy borrowing by individuals. They still don't understand today. It proved simple to engineer a regulatory over-response so that banks stopped lending even as the crisis deepened. We continue to encourage regulators to believe prudent regulation, formulaic box-ticking and legions of compliance and risk officers will avoid the crisis repeating itself.

It won't. A different crisis is guaranteed. The consequences of post crisis regulation are complex and have made markets substantially less efficient. These include:

- *Diminished liquidity across markets*
- *Devasted the effectiveness of global banking systems in allocating capital*
- *Transferred risk from highly experienced banks to unprepared fund managers – and spawned a host of failing lending vectors including crowd lending*
- *Caused a proliferation of wasteful, essentially bureaucratic roles and excessive reporting across banking*
- *Stifled financial innovation*
- *Decreased the access to capital for new and small businesses*

It is now necessary to have a degree in financial regulation before bankers even consider picking up the Financial Times each morning. Hamstringing the whole financial sector in red tape and regulation has been one of our most successful policies in making markets less efficient.

3) Austerity

Politicians have played their part. We managed to persuade global leaders to massively magnify the negative market effects triggered by QE and Over-Regulation by simultaneously enforcing **Austerity**. It's remarkable how policy makers did not seem to notice the contradiction between bailing out failed banks as central banks created billions via QE to drive growth, while they cut back spending on the real economy through "prudent" fiscal policy. It's little wonder the money all flowed into financial assets.

The result of 12 years of Austerity have been dramatic – essentially the once upwards evolution of society has split into a very small stream of increasingly uber-wealthy, and an ocean of less well-off who have seen their futures move into reverse gear:

- *Destabilised society, driving rising poverty, homelessness, depression and reducing life expectancies*
- *Stressed and decaying infrastructure ensuring long-term crisis,*
- *Strained social welfare networks, non-fit for purpose health and education services.*
- *Weaken confidence in political systems and solutions*
- *Failure to address employment needs in terms of changing global economy and innovate in terms of new tech (AI, 3D, Robotics)*

As incomes fell, welfare crashed, and inequality became increasingly apparent, we then entered a new exciting stage in our project:

4) Populism & Political Instability

Populism has been a tremendous success. Across the Western Economies we've seen an explosion in unsatisfied populations, rising dissent and the rejection of discredited political leadership. The *Gilet Jaunes* in France, Brexit in the UK and Trump in the US are all good examples. Some countries have swung to the left, others to the right, others want to split and fracture – we are pretty much indifferent, if they are divisive and loud. Local populist leaders have fuelled resentment over immigration, trade and wealth to garner support, further chipping away confidence. Free Trade was blamed, and protectionist policies enforced. These movements are founded in non-deliverable outcomes – which we of course encourage, secure in the knowledge they are unlikely to achieve much in the long-run beyond further destabilising sentiment.

In the short-term, the tensions they create feed into the project:

- *Totalitarism*
- *Distrust of Democracy*
- *Fractured Nation States*
- *Increased Discrimination: Racism, Bigotry, Sexism,*
- *Trade Wars and Protectionism*
- *The end of Free Trade and Economic Liberalism*
- *Exchange rate distrust*
- *Increased Global Conflict Threat*
- *Breakdown in International Cooperation*

Don't hesitate to ask if you have any questions.

TJ Wormwood

Lord 3rd Ring, 7th Circle.

CHAIN 6:

WTF is QE and Monetary Experimentation?

From: thedevil@hell.hel

to: tjwormwood@7circle.com

Subject: 5th Horseman – Explain QE Please?

TJ

There are a couple of things in your recent Mechanics of Global Financial Destruction Paper I'd like to understand better.

Let's start with QE. WTF is it?

Can you explain exactly what Quantitative Easing is? I need to understand it – doesn't make any sense to me. Explain how, what, why, the unintended consequences you refer to, and anything else I should know....

Do I mind dump on me...

NICK

From: TJ Wormwood, L3R7C

To: Lucifer, Lord of Infinite Darkness:

Subject: 5H – Explain Quantitative Easing,

FILE DOWNLOAD – Quantitative Easing and Monetary Experimentation

L'LOID

Quantitative Easing & Monetary Experimentation

This is some background on Quantitative Easing and Monetary Experimentation. Its deliberately complex – so let me try to cut through some of the themes.

The first thing is to understand QE is just one aspect of Monetary Experimentation. The great thing about monetary policy is Economists treat it as some kind of science, when its actually all about behaviour. When you start experimenting with monetary policy, the results can be very surprising indeed. But we didn't tell them that. Instead we encourage economists to focus on the details and let them assume monetary policy is predictable and scientific. The reality is its wonderfully chaotic, riddled with contradictory consequences and so complex few financial experts are able to perceive and compute the effects in whole.

My team and I are particularly thrilled about "QE". We think we may originally come up with the concept after a very liquid evening on Sake in a Tokyo strip bar many years ago when we persuaded the Bank of Japan that unlimited money creation couldn't fail to reinvigorate the moribund Japanese economy. They got a bit unhappy when we let on it was a bit experimental, so we thought up a serious sounding name: Quantitative Easing.

Giving financial concepts very serious sounding names is one of our tactics. It makes the concept sound very important and complex and triggers a "Emperor's New Clothes" syndrome moment – convincing folk to worry more about what they might not know, rather than question what they do know. The more complex something sounds, the less likely "financial experts" are to raise objections to it.

Since we suggested the idea, the Japanese government has been pumping money into its stagnant economy through the purchase of its own bonds, corporate debt and recently equities. They have been doing it for nearly 30 years. No one seems particularly bothered that it isn't working. Its even better than no one could explain how it should have worked, and even fewer can explain why it hasn't worked, or how the imagined and theoretical transmission mechanisms to drive growth fail!

QE has proved to be a wonderfully nebulous and obscure conceptual theory. We're absolutely delighted that every time a global recession threatens, market commentators now immediately assume we're in for more of it. Even though QE has proved such a stunningly unsuccessful and pointless exercise, nobody says so out loud. European growth slows so the ECB prescribes more of it. US picks a trade war, and the president starts screaming for lower rates to keep the growth level high.

Elevating QE to a semi-mythical status and ascribing it with magical money tree status, should make it a target. But it attracts little real criticism – probably because the regulatory repression of bankers makes everyone fearful for their careers. Fear has killed intellectual curiosity about financial markets. Traders don't really care – they know QE distorts markets by keeping rates too low, but why worry if prices are rising!

About the only thing people are certain about when it comes to QE is that it can be very successfully arbitraged. If governments announce they are going to buy back their own bonds, corporate debt or equity, then it makes absolutely perfect sense for investors to do exactly the same – coat-tailing governments, secure it's a trade pretty much guaranteed to make money and the government is there as a buyer when they want to sell.

Such arbitrage/follower behaviour largely explains the massive gains seen in the price of global bonds over the past seven years. Higher bond prices mean lower yields. Because markets are closely linked and price relative to each other, the distortions caused in one market push up prices quickly by percolating into other financial assets, driving the prices of all them higher. Therefore; QE has pushed interest rates lower and also driven up the price of shares. Its pure financial magic – and investors know it even though they don't quite understand how. QE has proved a rising tide that lifts all financial assets...

What happens when the tide goes out?

Since the crisis in 2008 investors have piled into financial assets. Which rather defeats the whole purpose of QE – which was intended to pump money into the real economy. Real Assets and Financial Assets exist in completely separate universes at present – a concept I will explain below. By piling into QE assets investors have not spent their money on building a stronger global economy based on new factories, better jobs, increased productivity or infrastructure.

The objective of QE was to stimulate the shocked post-GFC economy by reducing interest rates and pumping money into the monetary system in the expectation it would encourage investment across the real economy. The mechanism was for central banks to pump in the money by buying outstanding government bonds. Essentially it was a form of printing money. The theory was very simple – funds would then be encouraged to use that money to invest, creating employment and infrastructure, and strengthening the economy. We encouraged this view widely among central bankers and politicians as QE policy was being formulated.

The effect has been rather different.

Let's start with the Banks. They immediately optimised their capital. The capital rules – which weight risk – rank sovereign debt as zero risk. It was optimal for banks to take as much free money from central banks as possible, and then use it buy more and more sovereign debt, which they could then sell back the central bank in order to buy yet more sovereign debt. It's a wonderful process – they made repeat profits as rates fell and bond priced rose. More importantly, they didn't need additional capital. As interest rates the fell the banks and others made loads of money as the prices of their bonds rose.

However, as prices rose, the yield on government bonds fell. Investors who look to fund long-term liabilities and pensions found they could no longer meet their return targets. In order to raise returns, they initially switched from low risk government bonds, and went up the risk curve in search of higher returns. The economic optimisation objective for fund managers is to generate the highest returns for taking the least risk. QE changed that fundamentally. Investors started to "bar-bell": seeking higher returns by taking greater market risk, but, hedging their increased risk by buying yet more Government bonds!

Investors didn't take long to realise QE was a free and effectively unlimited option on all markets. Driving down interest rates drove up prices of all financial assets. Which is why global markets have thrived since the GFC even though the real economies in Western Economies such as the US, UK and Europe pretty much flatlined - trapped in a "new normal" slow-growth lower-for-longer interest rates mode. The stellar gains we've seen in stocks since 2008 simply aren't justified by the lethargic deflationary economic growth we've seen in these economies since the crisis.

Even though interest rates are now negative in many countries, investors are still buying negative yield government bonds because they perceive a clear arbitrage opportunity and a free hedge on renewed weakness – if central banks keep buying and easing rates, then investors can continue to coat-tail the gains these assets realise!

Knowledge based rational investment based on careful, considered and thorough due diligence of the market, business and fundamentals has gone completely out the window – investors now simply follow the QE buck! They are betting global central banks can't stop for fear of pricking the financial asset price bubble.

Then there is the ancestral memory of markets to consider. QE has been going for over 10-years. Most fund managers in the financial markets have never worked in anything but a falling interest rate environment. What will they do when if the tide comes in and interest rates rise? The older elephants in the investment herd have all been taken out! The young ones now assume QE is normal!

Markets are supposed to be about the most efficient allocation of scare resources. Or at least they are, right up the moment when they aren't... and the parameters change. Markets have become utterly distorted by QE.

There are many ways QE has altered the behaviour of market participants and triggered all kinds of unintended consequences.

Yield Tourism (i)

One of the major effects is yield tourism. When government bond yields fall to negative returns (as they have done), it becomes an enormous challenge for investors to meet their return objectives. You simply can't fund long-term pension liabilities from zero interest bond yields. $13 trillion of debt now trades at negative yields – about 40% of the total global bond market, creating a scarcity of positive bonds which in turn further drives up their prices, pushing more bonds into negative yields. It's yet another wonderful financial feedback loop. Falling bond yields mean investors have been forced to seek returns elsewhere, by climbing higher up the risk curve.

An investor who has happily been buying AAA rated risk-free Gilts (UK government bonds) starts to buy A rated corporate bonds because they yield more. But they are also more risky. Higher risk attracts a higher return. However, as every other investor is doing the same thing, then rising demand dictates the yield of an A rated bond will fall - to a level where it is no longer such a compelling asset from a return perspective. But it still yields more than Gilts, so investors buy them.

While sovereign borrowers generally don't fail, (unless its Argentina or Greece which will always default), single A rated issues do. If interest rates were to rise, it's extremely likely to cause the default rate of Single A rated issuers to rise, meaning rising rates represent massively increased risk for investors.

Yet, the same pension fund investors who once held government bonds, and are now the worried owners of A rated bonds, discover falling yields and lower interest rates mean their returns are still too low to meet their pension liabilities. So, they then must climb higher up the risk ladder and start buying sub-investment junk bonds to garner a similar return as they once got on the government bonds! The risk of a B- junk bond defaulting is substantially higher than a single A bond, and they are far more likely to fail if interest rates were to rise.

The end result of QE is that investors end up holding financial instruments that give little in terms of higher returns, are far riskier and less liquid. (Liquidity, or how easy it to sell a financial instrument, tends to get thinner and thinner as the underlying risk increases.)

"Take more risk to earn lower, less liquid returns" is not a recipe for investment success.

Yet, it defines the madness of the modern age. The investor does not fully appreciate just how illiquid till he tries to sell it and discovers there is zero bid. The markets are littered with examples of how liquidity is true slayer of funds and banks. When liquidity dries up, financial institutions die. Violently. Messily. Its marvellous.

Yield Tourism (ii)

But, wait! It gets even better and more complex.

Some investors might have spotted the soar-away stock markets and dividend yields, which normally lag bond yields, are now higher. They embark on long-distance yield tourism, and instead of buying nice predictable bonds, start buying equities. This particular investor may have understood investing in government bonds perfectly, which pretty much means he won't have a clue when it comes to investing in Equities. Bonds are defensive investments while Equities are aggressive.

Bond markets attract pessimists. They want to know how safe and secure their money is going to be in the event of inflation or a recession, and that they are going to get it back, even if the borrower fails. Bond Markets are based on common sense, careful analysis and seek dull, boring, predictable returns.

Equity markets are for optimists. Equity investors like stories, ideas, concepts and personalities. They gamble on risk. They are willing to invest on the basis of "careful and considered due diligence of market opportunities" which boils down to hunches backed up by a feeling it just might work. (Which, of course, then is backed up by pages and pages of balance sheet analysis, market and sector deep dives, and a full legal dissection of the opportunity to post-factually justify the hunch.)

The thing that makes Equities so dangerous is they attract bright, clever and imaginative people. Bright people with imagination don't get far in bond markets. Dull boring predictable clever ones do. Imagination is a terrible thing in bond markets....

Equities get very dangerous on the way up. Happy people at a party attract more happy people and more money. Stock markets go up because they attract more money, and because they are going up people put more money into them. And, if corporates are borrowing lots of money in bond markets and spending that money to buy back their own stocks, then the market goes up even faster, attracting even more money..... It's a fantastic positive feedback loop right till it snaps... which is when it starts raining bankers from tall buildings and the papers scream Financial

Armageddon.

As the market rises, the stock speculators find more and more reasons to buy. We even convinced them that making money isn't actually important for a stock to be valuable. It doesn't matter the company is never going to make a profit, because the bond market is lending it lots of money and the stock price is rising, therefore, (despite the fact it makes no profits, has missed all its sales projections and has half-a-dozen competitors chasing it), it is a screaming buy! Many of the Unicorn Tech companies will never ever make a penny profit – yet are still said to be worth billions!

Other forms of yield tourism include investors going higher up on the risk ladder by investing in subordinated capital instruments, derivatives, structured notes or onto to other branches of the financial risk tree by buying commodities. Each becomes more dangerous than the last. As more investors pile into new sectors in search of investment returns, every single financial asset class begins to exhibit distortion; resulting in lower returns, higher prices and higher risk. And, as they climb the ladder they know less and less about the assets.

It gets even more exciting. The higher an investor climbs up the Ladder of Risk, the less liquid the investments become. In times of financial stress illiquid assets become more and more sticky, and as already noted, more difficult to sell. In times of crisis, illiquidity sets like concrete. Investors can be trapped with unsellable assets, and an unsellable asset is valued at zero when the bailiffs are knocking at the door.

It's the "difficult to sell" bit that's really important. They day the New York stock exchange has 24 doors marked "Way In". There is only one marked "Exit". It can get very crowded if everyone tries to leave at the same time.

Financial Asset Inflation

As bond prices rise and stocks soar to stratospheric levels, maybe it's time to wonder about inflation? We did warn the potential consequence of QE would be inflation. Everyone agreed that printing lots of money through QE would generate inflation. Yet, it remains very low. All the central bank economists looking for inflation seem to have ignored the obvious place it's been hiding – financial assets!

It's pretty obvious why. All the money central banks printed through QE and supported by ultra-cheap interest rates remains and circulates within the financial markets and is invested in financial assets. QE money barely grazed the real world. Stocks are 200% higher since the crash. Yet, workers have seen their earnings fall in real terms, and have less to spend on the goods companies produce – that's a clear driver of deflation. If you are looking for inflation in the real economy, you are looking in the wrong place.

Corporate Borrowing

As interest rates fell to effectively zero, corporate executives and private equity owners realised they could effectively monetise their positions through leverage – borrowing money. Companies went out and borrowed trillions from the bond market (fuelled by yield tourists). They then didn't use that money for new Capital Expenditure; building new factories, plant, warehouses, infrastructure or creating jobs. Instead listed companies used most of the money to buy back their own stock – thus pushing up the stock price resulting in massive bonuses for company executives and windfall stock gains for owners. Private equity owners used debt to pay themselves massive dividends – converting equity into debt without diluting themselves.

Corporate stock buybacks add plenty to the wealth of shareholders and company executives, but add zero to the value of the company in terms of new productive capacity, productivity improvements or products! It's the most effective way we've discovered to channel the fruits of workers labour into the pockets of the management and owners. Capitalism at its finest.

Rising Income Inequality

As the value of financial assets rocketed and the owners became insanely wealthy, the optimism of equity markets ballooned. This was magnified in the tech sector where we managed to establish the Unicorn concept of tremendous and unlimited value in new disruptive stocks – even though experience shows very few new businesses aren't quickly arbitraged out by new-entrant competition, regulation and other factors, including the inability of many disruptive stock market darlings to actually deliver what they promised.

The fact a few Silicon Valley Tech Entrepreneurs now own unimaginable wealth while the City of San Francisco tumbles into decay, drugs, homelessness and poverty is a marvellous poster for rising income inequality, and the breakdown of paternalistic society. The rich have been very vocal about why they should not pay taxes to molly-coddle lazy workers, and that if they keep all their money, then it will trickle down through their spending and investments. Another gold-leaf flavoured Martini my dear?

We've managed to motivate and agitate the masses about the iniquity of income inequality, while keeping them distracted from the real dangers of QE in terms of financial growth vs real growth, while stalling real business investment and innovation.

Business growth

If you are the owner of a private equity fund with a host of companies in your portfolio, or the CEO of a leading company, then the way to maximise your economic return is simple. Leverage up by borrowing money in the bond market and using that money to push up the stock price of public companies or pay yourself greater dividends as a private company. Why take the risk of investing in capital expenditure on new business assets when the returns from stock buybacks are so simple?

When returns are so low, and risks so high, the prudent thing for corporates to do is not to invest in plant or productivity improvements. It's far too risky. Much better to spend their borrowed money by giving it to the owners or management.

To sum up:

QE has utterly distorted financial asset markets. By keeping interest rates artificially low, it has caused the price of all other financial assets to rise, even though productivity has barely improved and growth remains lacklustre. The result in inflation in the price of financial assets – which markets mistakenly perceive as profit. Its only profit if you can realise it by selling the asset.

The less obvious consequences of QE include massive distortions in investment and business behaviours, including companies leveraging up to borrow more to buy back their own stocks, which makes them more likely to go bust and leads to wider income inequality.

TJ Wormwood,

CDO – Fifth Horseman Project

L3R7C

CHAIN 7:

Now what is MMT?

From: thedevil@hell.hel

To: tjwormwood@7circle.com

Subject: 5th Horseman – I understand QE – but wtf is MMT?

TJ

Thanks for the run through on QE. I didn't ever grasp how distorting something like that would be. It does seem to have driven all kinds of unintended and danger consequences.

I note in the original paper you talked about MMT – Modern Monetary Theory? Could you explain this in some detail please?

Do a further mind dump on me..

NICK

From: TJ Wormwood, L3R7C

To: Lucifer, Lord of Infinite Darkness:

Subject: 5th Horseman – I understand QE – but wtf is MMT?

FILE DOWNLOAD – Modern Monetary Theory - MMT

L'LOID

Thanks for the reminder on Modern Monetary Theory. I have great hopes for it – but also some concerns. There is a possibility, just a possibility, that it might prove effective. I shall explain below...

As income inequality rises, financial assets rocket higher, the real economy stalls, and austerity wipes out social welfare, it's time to play the next card – political interference. We're giving politicians a weapon to address the social ills created over the past 10-years. We are calling it Modern Monetary Theory – "MMT". If we can get the electorates to continue blaming banks for the crisis and wonder at the inequity of bailing banks out with billions of dollars while they were punished through Austerity, then we can play a whole new monetary/fiscal game.

We came up with the MMT concept while idly wondering in meetings with central banks and earnest politicians why all the government bonds held by central banks couldn't just be written off?

If the Bank of England holds £40 billion of gilts, why not make them disappear? Why not? Effectively, these gilts are liabilities of the state, but as the state central bank is holding them at assets, then don't they nullify each other? Maybe even at a small profit to the bank?

After planting the idea in meetings with central bankers, politicians and radicals, we shut up and let them have their lightbulb moment as the idea took hold. The seed germinated. Now politicians are dreaming up massive spending plans with the free money we've persuaded them they invented. Central bankers are fretting about inflation, but we're subverting them on that as well – telling them the money already exists in the economy so how would it?

Although we've named it MMT, in reality its unconstrained fiscal spending wrapped in vague and unproven monetary theory. It looks cosmetically attractive and a solution.

We believe it's a trap.

We're confident it will trigger all kinds of unintended consequences, political shifts and insurrection, soaring wage demands, and collapse in confidence in government fiat money.

Let's start with Fiat Money. We've been encouraging the libertarian right wing and their agenda of non-state money by focusing them on "liberated" money through variations of crypto-currencies. We are very aware crypto-currencies are fraudulent tosh – but it's not our concern if folk want to believe in them because they are inherently greedy. We're now focusing them on the dangers of unconstrained government spending in terms of hidden state agendas and conspiracy theory! We're distracting them from the substantial corruption that is likely if Governments start to flow large state spending as contractors shave contracts and bureaucracies take their "share".

To be fair, MMT has some despicably good points – governments directly investing in the real economy through infrastructure projects, while social welfare programmes and education will do real good. Properly handled there is a possibility mankind could actually understand and control the risks of printing money and use the power carefully and well to reform health services, repurpose education, direct positive infrastructure projects, and combat mounting environmental and climate change dangers.

However, the stark reality is mankind is greedy and lacks the cohesion of purpose that would be necessary to redirect the global economy without getting it badly wrong.

If we get unconstrained MMT there is likely to be rapid inflation as money flows into the real economy and industry tries to play productivity catch-up. Concurrently, that will likely cause risk financial asset prices to fall as investors recognise the bubbles and try to exit – the very market crash Central Banks are trying to avoid.

MMT will drive politics, putting politicians promising high spending programmes into power – and vulnerable to corruption. Most importantly, it will further undermine confidence in fiat money. If governments truly can print as much money as they like – why shouldn't everyone get everything they want. The experience of high spending governments shows hyperinflation can occur frighteningly fast. Workers will demand higher and higher wages, demanding a greater share of the MMT spigot.

MMT raises a significant tax problem – why should billionaires pay any taxes if governments don't actually need their cash? What would they do with their money? Trickle-down is a libertarian myth. Invest alongside government, or do they take a lesson from history and seek to switch their money from the financial economy to the real economy – by selling stocks and bonds to buy bricks and mortar? That's a clear recipe for stock market meltdown and crisis, and a good reason for investors to buy non-financial assets.

We are extremely positive on the prospects for further monetary experimentation and MMT to further destabilise the global economy. There are risks, but the likelihood central banks and governments will be able to manage normalisation of interest rates, rebalance the financial and real economy, reconcile income inequality and solve a host of social and infrastructure issues is infinitesimally small.

TJ Wormwood

L3R7C

CHAIN 8:

Explain your problem with

Bureaucracy and Regulators

From: thedevil@hell.hel

To: tjwormwood@7circle.com

Subject: 5^{t}H - Can you give me your reasoning on Bureaucracy and Regulation?

TJ

The MMT sounds nicely insane. Can you really just create money like that?

I guess you can, but surely they must be aware of the consequences?

You have mentioned Bureaucracy a couple of times. Why are regulators an issue?

Do a further mind dump on me..

NICK

From: TJ Wormwood, L3R7C

To: Lucifer, Lord of Infinite Darkness:

Subject: Re: 5^{t}H - Can you give me your reasoning on Bureaucracy and Regulation?

Regulatory Overkill

Bureaucracy is a necessary evil – we love it. Regulation is a sub-branch of the bureaucracy genome.

Over the millennia we've encouraged, refined and nurtured bureaucracy as a true scourge of society. There is nothing quite so steadfast as a well-trained and determined bureaucrat determined the right form is filled in with the right boxes completed with the right coloured pen. It attracts individuals of a certain mindset. We encourage them to be diligent, focused and single-minded in their duties, because it frustrates everyone – especially entrepreneurs looking for profit.

While it is unlikely any child has ever consciously chosen their future path to be a bureaucrat – many societies greatly value sons and daughters with careers as civil servants or in office administration.

Bureaucrats tend not to get their primary satisfaction in life from the accolades and applause from their co-workers, praise for the quality of their insightful analysis, or even high salaries – which are limited in essentially administrative roles - but from their importance and place within the organisation. The economic goal of a bureaucrat is to maximise the range and scale of whatever it is they administer or claim responsibility for. For the true bureaucrat, the reward is years of steadily expanding oversight, and a good pension on retirement. To achieve these goals, they have to be diligent and effective.

Financial Regulators are a particularly refined and highly motivated cadre of specialized bureaucrats. They fill complex and demanding roles with little of the glamour and limelight that surrounds their charges; financial practitioners including bankers, traders and investors. They are highly educated, with minds trained to focus on detail and order. Yet, it is highly unlikely any finance graduate ever imagined themselves in a stunning, exciting, varied and remunerative career as a financial bureaucrat. Perhaps a few...

We've encouraged successful bankers to regard regulators as those who couldn't handle the pressure of the investment world. While Investment Bankers charge around the world finding new ways to bankrupt their clients and dreaming up increasingly complex ways to charge them excessive fees, financial regulators focus on the details of how banks should measure their capital and risk, account for disparities and report them (in green, blue or red ink). They analyse markets with care, consideration and at such a slow pace, bankers are left frustrated and flummoxed.

These attitudes breed resentment. Any financial regulator is just itching for the opportunity to stick it back to their financial charges.

Because they are fact, process and rules driven, and don't particularly care how markets work, financial regulators missed the signs of financial instruments overheating in the run up to 2007. They didn't spot the connections between declining lending standards, the packaging of debt into Asset Backed Securities, or connect the significance of how banks and investors legally hid their leverage and risk behind financial derivatives. The evidence was all there – one regulator fined a bank for predatory lending because it charged an unemployed bus driver more for a mortgage than it charged a hedge fund manager, while another threatened to take the same bank to court for unwise and careless lending practices when it followed the directions of the first regulator.

Financial regulation could be, and remains, a magnificently confusing and corroding minefield, only bettered by tax authorities.

Regulators struggled to understand what was going wrong when Global Financial Crisis first arrived in 2007. It took the initial form of funds being gated because the managers couldn't sell assets quickly enough to meet client demands for their money back. Which itself was due to the closure of commercial paper markets providing short-term funds triggering a liquidity crisis.

The crisis quickly accelerated away from them. We had the extremely satisfying sight of a full scale run on a UK Bank, which could have been so easily avoided if the Bank of England had a clue on the cataclysm of complex related events that were driving the financial system into meltdown. The collective confused reactions, and our encouragement, ensured the defining moment of the crisis, the collapse of Lehman Brothers, became inevitable.

Through the crisis regulators were generally ignored as long-term players and irrelevant in a crisis. Central bankers, government and bankers stuck the broken pieces of financial markets back together again and started to play the inevitable blame gain. Regulators saw the need to defend themselves and with surprising speed and alacrity, jumped in and redefined their role. They hastily designed and enacted a whole new set of regulations based on what they thought they knew about the crisis, with the aim of ensuring what they thought had happened never happened again. Of course, we ensured they were wrong in most of their assumed knowledge.

In their haste to maintain their relevance, these new rules weren't coordinated or optimised with the monetary inflation central bankers expected to create from QE. Neither were they closely aligned to efforts to stem the sovereign debt crisis, which was triggered by fears of over-indebtedness. Effectively, regulators regulated into a policy/crisis vacuum, unaware of the expanding ripples of crisis they were building around them.

As Central Bankers threw together QE with the aim of incentivising lending to business, Regulators were busily redefining capital rules to make it more costly and difficult for banks to finance companies. This triggered liquidity issues for property companies, small-to-medium sized enterprises (SMEs) and killed financial instruments that improved borrowing costs such as asset backed securitisation and derivatives.

The near death of the global banking sector in the wake of the Lehman collapse exposed significant capital mismatches at the major banks – which is hardly surprising as banks' capitalisation were simply optimisations of their risk and equity, which came undone during the crisis. (In 2006 Bank capital rules assumed financial institutions were far less likely to go bust than other corporates!)

Following the crisis, the Americans swiftly recapitalised their banking sector, forcing banks to reform and sort themselves. In Europe the sovereign debt crisis in the wake of the 2007 crisis successfully distracted attention from actually fixing broken banks. They remain broken. The unholy mess that is Italian Banking, and the financial monstrosities in Germany are among our finest creations.

Even as banks were trying to recapitalise, regulators stepped in to redefine what is and what is not capital, and decided it made sense to subordinate lenders to banks to equity holders. This was a fantastic piece of doublethink which we encouraged on the basis that since governments had had to bail out banks by taking all their equity, debt lenders had been barely inconvenienced. It made perfect sense to overturn 500 years of financial conventions, and to decree debt lenders would suffer equally in any future crisis. The concept of bailing-in debt lenders to collapsing banks was a truly inspired terrible idea. It significantly upped the uncertainty towards the banking sector in the post crisis markets.

Even better, as Bankers, Politicians and Central Bankers threw instruments of blame at each other, regulators found a fertile opening for new regulation. Since the crisis we've seen new regulations enacted in abundance disrupting every single niche of the financial markets.

The Science of Regulation is well defined – every action by regulators creates an equal and opposite reaction in the industry they regulate. This has spawned a massive growth in the compliance, risk control and monitoring and a whole ancillary business finding individuals qualified for these new niches. Salaries in these areas have ballooned, while bankers find their earnings dropping to pay for the reporting and compliance costs. Further resentment and less efficient financial services is the result.

Regulators reaction to the GFC was a plethora of urgent reactive regulations enacted across markets to address the risks they identified as having caused the crisis. The effects were multiple: clamping down on how bank capital was used to support trading, lending and investment, making investment more difficult, and even restricting the flows of information across the financial markets. It's now impossible for a financial analyst to give advice to a client unless the client is prepared to pay for it first. There are an increasing number of unemployed analysts.

We encouraged regulators to take the view that if banks stopped providing liquidity to markets, then markets would become less volatile. When markets don't trade, they can't crash!

We've further encouraged bank regulators to keep the banks distracted with repeated, and largely irrelevant, stress tests and constantly evolving and often contradictory rules designed to avoid a repeat of the 2007/8 crisis. The next crisis will be completely different, and they will miss the causes and effects again.

Regulatory failure since the crisis has created some very interesting opportunities to keep markets unstable and wrong footed.

Liquidity

Liquidity is the lifeblood of financial markets. Liquid markets are the ones where investors are most keen to transact, knowing they can get in and out of their investments. The financial markets once provided liquidity to markets – market makers providing two-way prices. This is no longer the case – market-making has died. The regulators hiked capital charges on trading positions to support market-making and later decided to regulate away any motivations for banks to make markets at all. There is now no market-making, just broking as traders try to match buyers and sellers. The result is the amount of capital employed by banks to provide liquidity to markets is about 10% of what it was in 2007.

Liquidity doesn't just kill banks like Lehman, Bear and nearly Northern Crock. It also kills investment managers who can't meet demands for cash returns from their investors.

The Banking System

A simple question on regulation since 2007 might be: Is the global banking system safer today than it was? The Regulators would argue it is – banks are subject to far greater oversight. Of what? Its' certainly true the banks now boast greatly expanded legions of compliance officers, risk managers and other forms of banking kommissars, but these people cost money. The competition to employ the best business prevention officers and risk dodgers has pushed up their salaries. That money must be found from somewhere – usually by dispensing with older, more expensive bank employees.

Whole cohorts of traders, salesmen, investment analysts, economists, treasury specialists, tax experts and banking experts have been …. "retired" since the crisis. They have been replaced with bright new fresh faced graduates encouraged never to learn the bad old ways of banking and embrace the new – whatever that might be in terms of regulatory tick-boxing. The genetic memory of banking has been dramatically cleaned out. And it will show when the next crisis inevitably occurs, and old lessons have to be relearnt.

It's not just bankers who changed, it's banking itself. Regulation and imposition of higher capital charges cut off lending to whole swathes of the economy. Following the crisis borrowers from property developers, small businesses and lenders found their access to banking services and capital slashed. They had to find new sources of capital. New funding conduits quickly emerged – for instance private debt, peer-to-peer lending and crowd-funding.

Anyone on a low income was stuffed as the banks turned them down and they were pushed towards an explosion of exploitative payday lenders willing to charge the poorest thousands of percent in interest. Most of the payday lenders are now bankrupted and gone, while the crowd-funders have bust after failing to manage credit risk on their lending platforms.

Nothing has yet truly replaced bank lending. As noted, crowd-funding and peer-to-peer markets looks increasingly wobbly. Direct lending by institutional investors has increased – many large funds are now active lenders to industry in both debt and equity – which is were we plan the next crisis. Banks once employed thousands of risk professionals who could identify and solve credit problems before and after they occurred. New institutional asset managers don't have the same risk genetic memory – 10-years ago the portfolio of an insurance company would largely comprise risk free US Treasury Bonds. Today it holds a portfolio of sub investment grade junk bonds, a negative yielding German Bund portfolio, and a portfolio of unlisted equity.

Where will they hide when the tide comes in?

Banking Innovation and Access

FINTECH, Digitisation and Platforms are the market buzzwords to describe how the financial industry is improving its "customer facing services". However, the range of investment products designed to provide better funding and investment solutions to clients is increasingly blocked. New rules on how issuers can securitise and secure their assets to improve funding costs have dramatically limited investment possibilities. Rules specify the kinds of risk investors may hold in their portfolios, while the business of investment analysis has been stifled by rules which means analysts may longer share their views and opinions lest it be construed as attempts to influence clients.

The result is a market far less rich with ideas and concepts to improve finance.

The ability of smaller firms to access the markets has largely been crowded out by the largest borrowers and largest investors. It's a simple rule of finance that it costs exactly the same to arrange and complete a $1 million investment as a $1 billion investment. As a result, no large investor can be "bothered" to look at any investments for, say, less than $100mm. When most small to mid-sized firms need smaller amounts to expand they find themselves stuck – outside the kind of small-scale low-risk business lending banks will now consider and too insignificant for the funds. They are essentially trapped.

The long-term consequences of over-regulation are far more pernicious than most market participants realise. Not only are markets less efficient, less well capitalised and less liquid, they are also lacking financial genetic memory, and are subject to overly complex rules. The ambition of markets to provide the most effective and efficient allocation of resources is compromised and wrapped in red tape.

TJ

_____From: thedevil@hell.hel

To: tjwormwood@7circle.com

Subject: Re: Re: 5^{t}H - Can you give me your reasoning on Bureaucracy and Regulation?

TJ

Fascinating. Bureaucracy as a necessary evil? How else would markets be constrained from misbehaviours if not by regulation?

NICK

_____

From: TJ Wormwood, L3R7C

To: Lucifer, Lord of Infinite Darkness:

Subject: Re: Re: Re: 5^{t}H - Can you give me your reasoning on Bureaucracy and Regulation

L'LOID

That's a great question, and one which the humans are beginning to answer for themselves. They are coming to understand how overly proscriptive rules get arbitraged by smart money trying to legally (and otherwise) get around them – which makes them less effective. They are also beginning to understand that simple less proscriptive principals are simpler to enforce, and more effective. The days of regulation for regulation's sake will end – but not yet.

In the early days of finance, participants were expected to play by the "unwritten" rules. If a market practitioner broke the rules, that news was quickly disseminated around all other participants, meaning the miscreants ability to transact again was severely limited. It was simple self-regulation of the market: break the rules and you are out. Over time the rules morphed into a trust and honour based system, but this was increasingly played by unscrupulous types looking for easy profits. As markets diversified and globalised the needs for rules became more obvious.

But complex rules are difficult to follow and difficult to police. Simple guidelines and rules utilise the market's ability to police itself through the value of participant's reputations, and simple rules about obvious illegal aspects of markets, such as front-running client orders, insider trading, fraud and financing terror, can be enforced. The optimal point is a free market with clear guidelines, an element of self-regulation, high standards and a few clear and simple rules. Legislating for every aspect of markets defeats its' primary purpose: efficient allocation of capital.

Let me give you an example of over-legislation: Mifid II, a collective set of rules intended to create greater transparency in markets, lower costs, better execution and improve market behaviour. One of the aspects was to outlaw companies offering free research to their clients on financial investments in case it unfairly "induced" them to trade with them.

The results have done nothing to improve markets. The unintended consequences include reducing the amount of knowledge available to potential investors, turning knowledge into a commodity only the rich can access, and killing research completely on smaller companies, essentially making their access to markets more difficult and more expensive.

The regulators think they have "reduced conflicts of interest, improved accountability and produced cost savings for investors." The reality is the rules have made it more difficult for investors to find information and research, it has concentrated the business in fewer larger firms, made information an expensive commodity by pushing up investor costs, while diminishing the access of smaller companies to the markets.

We can consider such pointless and damaging financial regulation – which cost the financial services industry billions to put in place – a stunning success in making markets less efficient.

Yours

TJ

L3R7C

CHAIN 9:

Austerity? How does that relate to the Global Financial Crisis?

From: thedevil@hell.hel

To: tjwormwood@7circle.com

Subject: 5^{t}H - Austerity? How does that relate to financial crisis?

TJ

You credit governments with supporting our programme through Austerity spending – which I assume means spending less? How can they be spending less when it seems Central Banks have been spending trillions?

NICK

_____

From: TJ Wormwood, L3R7C

To: Lucifer, Lord of Infinite Darkness:

Subject: Re: 5^{t}H - Austerity? How does that relate to financial crisis?

L'LOID

Very astute observation.

Austerity is one of the key issues we encouraged to drive the Global Financial Crisis. As the globe went into recession following the crisis, we were able to persuade governments to adopt pro-cyclical policies, cutting back spending to match reduced tax incomes and avoiding too much debt.

This was a long-term concept we'd introduced into politics back in 1979 when Mrs Thatcher persuaded the electorate that in times of financial crisis, it's a natural and right reaction to tighten one's belt a few notches and prepare for leaner times. It's a very human reaction, but not necessarily the one even a minimally competent government should take.

Immediately following the Global Financial Crisis we'd helped to engineer, we directed our efforts at maintaining uncertainty, keeping governments unstable, and sought to direct them down the wrong routes - including a collective tightening of their belts – even as the global economy was in freefall.

If mankind ever gets down to analysing what happened during the GFC, they will likely conclude it was flawed policy responses that made it so deep and damaging. It will take them years to work it out. Eventually, they will wonder - with some bafflement - why nations adopted as destructive a policy as Austerity in the wake of the most damaging peacetime economic slowdown. Immediate counter-cyclical government spending would have been far more effective.

The financial crisis began in 2007 and quickly evolved way past a once in a decade stock market collapse. It became the deepest global financial crisis on record. It nearly brought down banking systems in the US, UK and parts of Europe. It reached its crescendo with the collapse of Lehman Brothers in 2008, before morphing into a European sovereign debt crisis. The crisis still reverberates, and periodically reignites around markets.

The immediate consequence of the Lehman collapse was a dramatic collapse in confidence across economies. Business travel crashed, companies undid expansion plans, projects were shuttered. Nearly every single global economy experienced a stall-speed event. Confidence in growth was shattered. Confidence in the future evaporated.

Governments faced sudden and enormous crisis: did they let banks fail and collapse? That could have caused dramatic systemic crisis across economies if bank failure plunged economies into freefall as banking systems failed. The connectivity between banks in terms of complex derivative contracts, intrabank lending and cross holdings meant one bank failing would likely cause others to topple like a massive game of Jenga.

The solution was a massive bailout of the global banking sector – which, cosmetically, cost governments billions of dollars. That was followed by massive intervention by Central banks to cut interest rates and flood economies with liquidity – ultimately in the form of new money though QE and asset purchase programmes.

As we've seen, these didn't quite work out as expected.

Central Banks pumped liquidity into the system. But that liquidity ultimately benefited only the financial system. The expected transfer mechanisms that would have pumped excess liquidity from banks into the real economy didn't happen. Banks were essentially closed to new lending – from mortgages (which exacerbated a property crash) to business lending, which deepened the slowdown.

Following the banking crisis, nervous investors looked for next thing to break – and they quickly identified burgeoning government debt as the most likely vector of future crisis. The vast amounts of money being doled out to banks, and the scale of losses awakened fears governments simply couldn't bear the costs. Faith in governments had been battered by the crisis, and by the sheer scale of bank bailouts countries had been forced to undertake. Some small counties, notably Ireland and Iceland, came perilously close to collapse as their bloated international banking sectors crashed and required massive costly bailouts.

The scale of global bailouts had been immense. That left investors wondering how good the credit of sovereign nations really was, and if they could stand it. It's a long-held belief Sovereign states can't go bust – after all, they have the keys to the printing presses to repay their debt by printing more cash. Typically, printing money causes inflation. When sovereigns go broke, its usually because they have liabilities in other currencies, which are dramatically magnified if/when their domestic currency collapses as a result of inflation. (Argentina is a good example – borrowing in dollars which it is repeatedly unable to repay.)

Governments know the importance of the investors who fund their government debt. To convince them they were safe and secure, satisfy their credit tests, and to demonstrate their fiscal probity and prudence, they immediately promised to scale back government spending, balance their books, and trim their debt deficit funding. European countries had already promised to stick to strict German mandated Debt to GDP ratios, but nobody had paid any attention to these agreements' pre-crisis. If fact some countries, including France, Italy and Greece had deliberately fiddled their debt to GDP numbers to meet the test criteria, assisted in some cases by our agents at the investment banks.

Following the crisis and bank bailouts, doubts about the scale and sustainability of sovereign indebtedness quickly became a secondary crisis in Europe. European countries don't own their own money printing machines anymore – (although we think the Italian have probably stashed a few away for the coming rainy days.) They gave up their monetary independence to the ECB and the almighty Euro. The global perception was European countries owing money in Euros would find themselves in all sorts of trouble, with many heading towards default.

It soon became clear weak European credits, particularly Greece and Portugal, had been borrowing way beyond their means, and way beyond the allowances specified by European rules! Ireland had effectively spent its entire rainy-day fund and more rescuing its over-levered and frankly stupid banks. All European economies were in thrall to the more productive and efficient Germany. As a result, confidence in Greek debt and the country went into freefall, triggering a systemic widening of government debt spreads across Europe – most damaging across the Southern European peripheral nations and Ireland. Bond yields soared to unsustainable levels as investors anticipated the likely default of several struggling Euro members becoming a full Euro collapse.

European sovereigns didn't break and default – mainly due to the efforts of the ECB and its president Mario Draghi who swiftly shored up ailing banks and directed them to fund sovereign debt. With the exception of Greece, which became and remains a political problem, European government yields started to fall, tightening relative to Germany.

The fears and doubts about the scale of government debt and the likelihood of default turned out to have been seriously overexaggerated by the markets. But we didn't know that at the time. Although the whole global economy was still mired in the aftershocks of the Lehman collapse and the financial crisis, and was desperately in need of fiscal boosting, global governments had committed themselves to cutting spending and Austerity.

For the purposes of bringing down the global economy, it was pretty perfect. The exhausted and battered global economy dragged itself out through a faltering, stuttering long drawn out slow wheezing recovery. The expected strong recovery and inflation never materialised. It was the called the new normal – low rates and low growth. Despite the low interest rates fostered by global QE, and all kinds of efforts to stimulate activity, the Occidental economies remained anaemic. Post crisis unemployment, especially youth unemployment, remained stubbornly high in many countries.

With the benefit of hindsight, it's clear the Western economies needed some extra fiscal juice from counter-cyclical spending to recover – which Austerity denied!

The effects have been dramatic:

The Wealth Consequences of Austerity.

Despite the amount of cash printed to finance QE and the Financial Asset sector, the money was too tight to mention when it came to government spending on the real economy. This is an important moment: while it was ok for Central banks to print unlimited amounts of money to inflate the value of financial assets, it was most certainly not ok for governments to print money to create real jobs and employment investing in the real economy. A cynic might say governments turned a blind eye to the rich getting richer on financial asset inflation, while generating deflation in the real world, making the poor much poorer.

Instead, government spending was cut to persuade investors to keep buying government debt – another moment of blessed ignorance. These same investors were proving more than willing to buy government debt because they were coat-tailing the central banks who were buying it under QE programmes! Another feedback loop.

Another issue is government revenues – the ultra-rich pretty much decided they didn't need to pay taxes, so they started to put dividends and income offshore, secure in the knowledge domestic tax collectors would ignore them as too difficult to enforce action upon. (It's far easier for tax authorities to hound a grocer owing £100 into an early grave than it is to get billionaire to pay a penny.) The rich argued their wealth would trickle down to the poor in the form of spending, their entrepreneurial talents creating new and better jobs, and investments. It is bunkum, but it remains undisputed truth for the right-wing in the US.

There are too many instances to cite of how spending cuts cut hope. As the global economy flatlined and crime rose, police forces were cut. As job related mental illness rises, care programmes are closed. Workers' rights are ignored, and the gig economy holds them to ransom working for longer hours, less pay and zero security. Resentment breeds resentment.

Social Cohesion

If all the goods and assets of human society were shared equally, then everyone would be a millionaire. But life is inherently not fair. Some have the ability to thrive and earn a larger share, while others do not. Social Darwinism dictates the strong survive and weak suffer, but over the last 200 years the increased cohesion of society has put in place welfare programmes to protect and nurture the weak.

It's a justifiable progression and proposition – social cohesion is as much a Public Good as clean water, a healthy environment or collective defence. A socially cohesive society is wealthier and less likely to revolt – which is why high welfare provision societies in Scandinavia tend to be happier, healthier, wealthier and live longer. (We've tried to stamp it out, but the Nordics are protected by the Asgardian Faction who have a particular soft spot for that part of the world.)

Elsewhere, we've been able to use Austerity to inflict massive social pain and general unhappiness: cutting welfare budgets across the globe and fuelling resentment.

A great example of Austerity Failure in Action is San Francisco:

> Its perhaps the most beautifully situated American City. Stunning architecture and marvellous views. Its home to 5 of the 10 richest people on the planet. It's the centre of Silicon Valley and the home of the Tech Revolution.

> It's a truly miserable place.

> Nearly every major street hosts a tented village of homeless hopeless vagrants, drug abuse is apparent everywhere, untreated mental illness stalks the streets, which are caked in human waste. Yet, it has the highest house prices in the US, gated communities for well-heeled tech execs, the most expensive shops, and best paid jobs. The rich never even con-

sider public transport when they can order an Uber or Lyft in seconds.

Speak to the rich residents and they don't even realise they have a mass social disease. The rich don't notice, and the poor are invisible. Write about it and be trolled. Attempts to solve it are shouted down as "socialism". National politicians berate each other for the failure to cure such deprivation across the US – but then play political games to cut the healthcare and social programmes that could resolve it.

Much of the social crisis created by Austerity could be cured through the innovation of new social policies that focus on welfare, quality of life and care provision. But they never will... it's too difficult.

A classic single point example of austerity thinking is tax collection. Its unthinkable for a national tax authority to take on a global corporate behemoth. The corporate can afford to spend millions on tax-lawyers and tax-constructs to avoid paying billions in taxes. Tax authorities know it's a pretty pointless exercise to go after them, it would be costly and unproductive when what's really required is a complete and considered reboot of tax codes and tax law. Such a reboot would also be costly and require complex negotiations between the bureaucracies in charge to ensure no loss of oversight. (As such, we've proven it's bureaucratically impossible to actually change tax law.)

Instead, the tax collectors go after the low hanging fruit. While a major internet click and deliver entity pays not a single penny in tax, tax collectors are incentivised to hound small businesses and individuals for relatively small sums. The costs of such polices likely outweigh the tax recoveries made – but they keep the tax bureaucracy busy and relevant.

Austerity doesn't hit evenly across society – as I noted earlier, it barely grazed the wealthy.

Infrastructure

The economies of the West are tired and broken. For instance, the railways in the UK are still running on essentially 180 year old tracks and signalling while US roads are unfit for purpose with a massive backlog of foregone maintenance. Infrastructure spending on hospitals, schools, ports and other necessities would provide another real economic boost. But it's not only mired in financial concerns but also bureaucracy and the difficulty of forcing through meaningful change.

The key issue about infrastructure isn't the past – it's the future. The Occidental economies of the US, UK and Europe are variously setting up for the coming trade conflict with China. Yet China has built more roads in the last 10-years than every other country through history, has invested heavily in new rail and air infrastructure, created new effective education networks and is now building global trade links.

Ask any bank analyst who will win the coming trade war, and they will probably answer the West. Why? Apparently, the west is better educated, more innovative, has won more Nobel prizes, is free and able to export and redefine global supply chains, while China is an authoritarian state entity trapped in limited thinking. It's a view we encourage because its' stupid.

The reality is China may be authoritarian, but its fresh, ready and willing and works! The West is tired and old, mired in economic despondency, decaying infrastructure, an addiction to decaying welfare services that are at least 50 years past their reinvention dates, and in thrall to state-capture by empowered bureaucracies.

> For instance, the UK's National Health Service has faced a massive bed-blocking crisis that gets worse every year as an aging population can't be found care elsewhere. The bureaucracy that runs health keeps spending but hasn't invested in solutions. Nor have they persuaded government a root and branch reboot of age-related welfare is required – because

that might involve discussions on reallocating their current budgets. So, the NHS keeps filling expensive high-tech hospital beds with elderly patients rather than building effective, comfortable but low-tech care and rest homes for them to recover in.

Infrastructure is not an easy spend. The experience of collapsing "infrastructure project management firms" in the UK highlights the risks. Large firms managing delivery of high cost government projects going bust on managerial and cost control failures? And government spending tends to involve a certain amount of corruption in the allocation of contracts and kickbacks.

The New Economy and Education

Among the great contradictions of Austerity is Education and the New Economy

The future economy is going to be dramatically different from today. Automated factories, artificial intelligence, nanotechnology, 3D printing and a host of new technologies are poised to provide high paying jobs, quality lifestyles, health and welfare improvements and increased leisure time. The range of environmental problems to be addressed and solved is enormous – removing plastic from the oceans and carbon dioxide from the atmosphere. Solving these issues is possible and should be probable. The sky is no longer the limit: the possibilities for mining asteroids and building industrial production facilities in orbit is technologically feasible.

These are not threats. These are opportunities.

Of course, we paint these opportunities in purely negative Luddite terms – how Robotics will create mass unemployment, AI will enslave workers, nanobots will grey-goo the planet, space is an expensive science-fiction distraction, while denying the planet is environmentally stressed.

The most important factor for an economy to succeed in developing the opportunities of the coming modern age will be the availability and quality of an educated workforce. They need to be training the engineers, the health care professionals, the designers and managers of the future economy today.

Instead, austerity means politicians have cut funding to Education from the bottom up. Larger class sizes in primaries ensure schoolkids can barely read, write or count when they progress to pack-em-in comprehensive secondary schools, where their learning options are increasingly limited through cutbacks and cost savings, and a general societal indifference to education because populations have been led to perceive a pretty dystopian future with limited opportunities to better themselves. (There is, of course, the very expensive option of private education for the elites - a privilege of wealth, not ability.)

And, to complete the undermining of the whole basis of education, we then charge students ruinous fees to attend second and third-rate courses at underperforming universities in courses will little real-life application or work relevance. The world can only use so many "business", "leisure" or "media" study graduates. Education is not planned or focused to produce the highly qualified degree level technicians and specialists we need for the new economy.

Instead we charge students to give them limited knowledge and unusable skills, handicap them with a debt millstone, and present them limited life opportunities. Their outlook is limited – with few expectations of owning their own home, or even a family life and kids they can enthuse about the future. The misery quotient rises and the dream off the new economy remains just a dream.

Through history Education has proved itself the most important factor in raising the level of human prosperity. What better way to limit the future than by destroying it? Some foolish politicians ask what is the wasted cost of educating the population if they end up leaving the country. The correct answer should be: what is the cost of not educating them and they stay?

What can we conclude about Austerity? It's been a tremendously efficient way of holding back economic growth and innovation at the social level, while also breeding serious discontent. As the decaying economies of the west crash into a diminished future, what's the likely outcome? Resentment, isolationism and increased protectionism. The prospects for a new dark age are promising.
TJ

From: thedevil@hell.hel

To: tjwormwood@7circle.com

Subject: 5^{t}H - Austerity? How does that relate to financial crisis?

TJ

Steady! You are beginning to sound a little bit like these unkempt socialists we've got caged on the 5th floor.

I get austerity. It works. To keep it going we have to keep governments scared of raising debt to finance recovery?

NICK

From: TJ Wormwood, L3R7C

To: Lucifer, Lord of Infinite Darkness:

Subject: Re: 5^{t}H - Austerity? How does that relate to financial crisis?

L'LOID
That's about it. Stop them from spending, keep their economies broken and their people starved of services!

TJ

CHAIN 10:

Politics? What can possibly go wrong?

From: thedevil@hell.hel

To: tjwormwood@7circle.com

Subject: 5^{t}H - Politics? What can possibly go wrong there?

TJ

I've never been a particular fan of this democracy nonsense, but you seem to think it's a plus factor in creating instability. Please expand?

NICK

_____

From: TJ Wormwood, L3R7C

To: Lucifer, Lord of Infinite Darkness:

Subject: Re: 5^{t}H - Politics? What can possibly go wrong there?

L'LOID

Populism and Political Instability

My Lord, Democracy is a marvellous concept – giving people the right to think they have a say in their society makes it increasingly difficult and complex to agree on any solutions. Populism and ongoing Political Instability is the fourth strategy we've pursued.

Our goal is simple: If political figures can't lead, then they can't identify, address and certainly not solve problems. We've achieved success across our target economies by destabilising and undermining confidence in traditional politics and political leaders – a surprisingly easy proposition. Our efforts have been supported by the unintended consequences we foresaw from the Global Financial Crash in terms of declining living standards, falling real wages, and resentment over rising income inequality. We've spiced it with flavours of fake news and social media.

It's helped that 30-years of largely anodyne social democracy since the end of the last cold war has dulled the political senses and ambitions of the democratic nations. The electorates have become more and more concerned with their perceived rights rather than what is possible. We've seen a series of increasingly grey and lacklustre leaders of diminishing stature presiding across the Occidental nations. Politicians may come from the same backgrounds as before, but they've gone from being respected "fathers of the nation", to celebrity figures worthy of national derision.

Political power has swung from wage-seeking organised labour leaders playing the most significant role in government calculations, to government now pandering to tax-avoiding job-creating "entrepreneurs". Through the 1970s-1990's union leaders were instantly recognisable national figures, while business leaders were largely unknown. Today, labour leaders are faceless, and the cult of business rules supreme. Start a tech firm, wear a black polo-neck, raise billions and you can command a far stronger social-media following than any politician.

Or claim to be a billionaire entrepreneur, star in your own TV programme lauding your self-declared business acumen, then get elected to the most powerful job on the planet without any definable or measurable political skill or background. We really could not have made that one up! Celebrity politics has become a career choice.

Its unlikely we'll see political power ever revert to organised labour – centre and right-wing governments have strengthened legislation designed to constrict the unions power. By neutering the workers, political power now follows economic power -

which resides with the suits (or actually, people so powerful they don't even have to not wear a tie.) The result is weak government across the democratic nations.

A consequence of weakened politics is bureaucratic control of the state has become more concentrated in the hands of civil servants. Bureaucrats don't hand back control – they retain it by keeping politicians weak and uninformed, which is best achieved by telling them how clever and powerful they are.

A remarkable number of counties seem to survive periods of non-political leadership without government, being run on a care-taker basis by their civil servants. In 2010 Belgium managed without a functioning Government for 541 days, and absolutely no one noticed the difference!

As the importance of real politics diminished, the Politics of Frustration and Protest became more influential. Brexit is a great example of the politics of frustration – UK voters being frustrated by what they perceived as Europe meddling in British laws. We've successfully used Brexit to fuel populism across the Occidental economies. Frustration and dissatisfaction created a fertile ground for multiple variations on Protest Populist politics.

Populism is a marvellous political disruptive movement – creating massive distraction and leaving politics rudderless. Surprisingly, one of the most attractive features of populism is how short-lived it tends to be. Waves and wave of populism occur, but when they get elected to power, they seldom survive... coming apart on their lack of strategic planning and vison, limited objectives and unrealistic expectations, leaving power vacuums in their wake.

For economies to move forward they need shared objectives and common purpose as citizens acknowledge and accept the state's aims and objectives. So, lets ensure no one can agree.

Brexit as a Populist Case Study

The Brexit vote was a staggering success in terms of populism and breaking the political consensus. For 380 years – since the English Civil War, British politicians have governed within fairly narrow bands where it was easy for participants to pick and choose, agree or disagree and switch if required. Politics could be angry and contentious, but seldom binary.

In Brexit we found a way to disrupt and create an arbitrary binary divide through society – Leave or Remain - and exploit it. The task was to frame a question for a referendum no one could avoid except in purely binary terms – In or Out. We had to build the case, fanning resentment of European meddling in domestic issues, building a narrative about wasteful Brussels salaries while hinting at corruption, playing to themes such as the immigration threat, perfidious Johnny Foreigner, and the banned bent banana story.

Perhaps our greatest contribution to the Brexit vote was persuading the BBC to show near constant repeats of Dad's Army, a 50 year old TV comedy about Britain standing alone against a hostile world, and for the commercial channels to repeatedly show black and white war films about plucky Brits bashing the Bosche.

Then, of course, we told outright lies through the referendum campaign, and still surprised ourselves by winning. It didn't actually matter that we did. Had the Leave side lost, they'd be screaming foul and demanding their right to a second vote! The Brexit referendum has effectively undone consensus politics in the Britain. Its either Leave or Remain. Are you a Cavalier or Roundhead? There is not a middle ground. You can't be a little bit leave just as you can't be a little bit pregnant.

Politics in the UK is now binary and divisive. It will take distracted years to rebuild confidence in politics and undo the damage. The result is a country unable to find a simple democratic parliamentary majority to agree the UK's terms of Brexit exit. Years of distraction from real political issues while political parties unravel.

Job done.

Europe

In France, we managed to wipe out the established political classes by engineering a sweeping victory for the deeply flawed, but young and earnest Emmanuel Macron's En Marche, giving French voters a simple choice: elect him or elect right-wing extremists. He won. We then gave Macron just enough time to make himself massively unpopular before further destabilising the country as the anti-government Gilet Jaunes swept onto the scene, the Champs-Elysees and everywhere else. Their agenda is not much more that not liking government, but it's enough. They are as revolting, in the nicest possible sense, just like the Far Right which promises a French solution to each and every economic and social ill – blaming immigration and the EU. It all keeps France politically volatile, and forces Macron to demonstrate leadership by picking a fight with his former BFF Angela Merkel.

In the autumn years of Merkel's chancellorship, Germany is consumed by a sense of wretchedness about its relevance. In the old East its crystallised into the classic right-wing agenda of blaming immigration for everything. In the West, Germany blames Europe for their woes, and can't really understand why everyone resents the success they are making of the new Europe. As consensus unwinds around the increasingly Learesque Merkel, populism is supporting conflicting Green and Right-Wing agendas, and distracts her from the manifest destiny/long held goal of ensuring German's rightful position running the controlling organs of the emerging European super-state – preferably from Berlin.

Italy and the rest of Europe are just noise. Italy being a curious right-wing/left-wind anti-establishment mix that will spontaneously combust at some point soon. The Balkans are Balkanised.

The Poles are showing the proverbial finger to European Law. The rest of Europe can't decide where they lie.

The result is Europe refocused inwardly, on domestic politics not policies, at a time when it desperately needs to solve the instability created by the Euro. One of the more intellectual arguments we used to win the Brexit referendum was Europe's likely collapse due to the Euro. We argued the Euro was a purely monetary construct without a solid fiscal agreement – financial union – to back it up. Any sane analysis would conclude the UK should exit to avoid being sucked in. To keep the argument fresh, we make sure we fund the Remainers to bleat and groan about how terrible an exit will be.

10-years after the global financial crisis, there is the ongoing economic misery across Europe. The European economy remains stalled – and there are signs it could get worse, especially in Germany if the global economy slips into a protectionist recession. It looks likely the ECB will have to resume QE and cut rates just to slow recession. The protectionist policies of the new US means it is also likely Brexit will result in Europe becoming increasingly insular, detached and delinked from the US and other Occidental economies, and irrelevant to the growth economies of the Orient.

It's critical we ensure it happens – by reawakening and encouraging hostility between France and Germany and ensuring the real European issue – solving the economic problem of the Euro by pulling together fiscal union, a growth agenda, agreeing how to reflate deflationary economies, and preparing for Post-Brexit Europe- and all these issues are left unaddressed by the complex EU autocracy.

The US

Surprisingly, populism in the form a popular outspoken TV personality looks likely to be long-lived. He has proved so divisive to the political classes the democrats are hurling themselves lemming-like at him rather than working on the policies needed to counter him. His own party sits in shocked horror at what he's doing, but they roll with it despite his bad, because he's their bad!

Trump has been tremendously successful in our facilitating our long-term populist objectives; the collapse of confidence in democratic government, undoing international trust, protectionism and driving trade and shooting wars. Under his watch, the US looks more authoritarian today than at any time in its recent history. It encourages totalitarian states by offering to deals with them – albeit on Trump's terms. Embracing the concept of trickle-down economics from the rich as established an oligarchy of wealth within the US – maybe not from illegal activities, but as pernicious in terms of the damage to society.

The destabilisation of politics and the cult of populism is a critical piece of the jigsaw for ensuring ongoing uncertainty and confusion.

TJ

CHAIN 11:

Europe and the UK? Please explain?

From: thedevil@hell.hel

To: tjwormwood@7circle.com

Subject: 5^{t}H - Politics? Europe vs UK? Please explain ?

TJ

Ok – get that. However, I'm a bit unclear about this Europe business. I always try and watch the BBC News to find out what **Hemself** is thinking, and I can't quite understand why the Brits are so vehemently pro or anti Europe.

But what really confuses me is Europe itself? I though they all hated each other but Europe seems quite a strong concept?

Can you put me right here?

NICK

—————————————————————————————————————

From: TJ Wormwood, L3R7C

To: Lucifer, Lord of Infinite Darkness:

Subject: Re: 5^{t}H - Politics? Europe vs UK? Please explain ?

L'LOID

Another great question. Its not so much a matter of the UK, but of Europe. We've done a cracking job in the UK fermenting European aggravation. A large slice of the British middle class believes we should stay in Europe, while the lower orders buy into the Johnny

Foreigner being here to nick their jobs, fornicate with their wives and steal their cars. The truth is the other way around!

But let's start with Europe.

A united Europe is a pretty good idea – and therefore one we don't wish to promote. For the last 3000 years the continent has been criss-crossed by disparate demented separate tribes fighting and slaughtering each other. Over the last 500 years it developed into 4 main groups:

- The Brits – Who pretty much kept to themselves and looked elsewhere except when one of the others looked likely to get too dominant.
- The French – Who were kept to themselves by dint of being at the centre and upsetting everyone else.
- The Spanish – Who discovered gold in the Americas and promptly bankrupted themselves morally and economically, and
- The Germans – Who were happy slaughtering each other until the coalesced into a single state united around a new shared common goal to beat up the French or anyone else if the French weren't available..
- Other players included Italy, Russia and a few others who are outside this quick and simple explanation.

By the last century power plays in Europe were largely between France and Germany while the UK playing a bemused cousin trying to keep the peace, but far more interested in the global empire it had acquired for itself while Europe battered the crap out of itself for the 300 preceding years.

After a couple of World Wars even the UK was exhausted and it was generally agreed it would be a pretty good thing if Europe all played nice with each other and teamed up to cooperate rather that annihilate each other, and the concept of European Union was launched. The project quickly took on a life of its own – spawning its own Brussel's bureaucracy and a hybrid political structure that quickly perceived the need to make Europe relevant to the citizens.

We have set out to undermine all the various positive elements of Europe and the Euro. We've implanted doubts on the political motives of the European Union, trying to destabilise it through Franco/German friction. We've launched projects to divide any unity of purpose by questioning whether such disparate European tribes really share any common shared goals and culture. We've exaggerated differences between the nationalities to stir up distrust and contempt – painting Germans as nasty, French as arrogant, Italians as lazy and Greeks as Greeks. In this department we've worked especially hard to destabilise the Euro, painting it as unworkable and against the interests of all members except Germany.

The truth about Europe is mixed. Yes, there are significant cultural differences and attitudes towards work, but if the ECB and EU can agree a common fiscal union to match the ECB monetary union, and support this Europe wide, then there is really no reason the Euro and Europe can't work. Its clear a majority of Europeans agree – especially the younger ones. Its therefore our job to make sure it doesn't happen.

TJ

CHAIN 12:

What if this doesn't work, and it backfires against us?

From: thedevil@hell.hel

To: tjwormwood@7circle.com

Subject: 5^{t}H - What are the risks it backfires against us..

TJ

Right, I think I grasp the key concepts here. Its all interconnected. The Global Financial Crisis of 2007 onwards has been exacerbated by bad monetary policy in the form of QE, poor regulatory choices, government mistakes on Austerity financing, and the unravelling of political confidence. I think I know enough now to push these to the DAB.

Are there any risks that you are making things so bad it actually works in mankind's favour?

NICK

From: TJ Wormwood, L3R7C

To: Lucifer, Lord of Infinite Darkness:

Subject: Re: 5^{t}H - What are the risks it backfires against us..

L'LOID

Let me give you an example of why this isn't going to sort itself out.

As I've noted several times, we've managed to create a space/time/reality rift between the deflating real world economy and the inflated price of financial assets. In any normal reality, the laws of consequence would dictate a correction. Given the geo-political crisis we're creating with trade wars and protectionism we'd expect a massive stock market crash followed by global recovery and interest rates rising to real numbers a point or so above inflation. Under such "normalisation" there would be pain in stocks and later in bonds.. but long-term the Global economy would pick itself up and march forward.

This time it's different.

This time Global Central Banks have given a "put" to the entire Financial Asset Market. They can't afford or face the prospect of bursting bubble in Bond or Stock Markets. It would send such a wave of poor sentiment and systemic financial mayhem around the globe that markets would be even more shocked and damaged by the 2008 Lehman moment. Moreover, it would confirm the decisions made by regulators, central banks and governments over the last 12 years have been hopelessly mistaken. For that reason, and perhaps for that reason alone, a major market crash is unlikely to happen. Global central banks will keep pumping free money into financial assets in the desperate and unlikely hope either inflation or global growth catches up – which is definitionally a bad strategy because they've been waiting for the last 10-years for it to happen.

Our programme of ongoing financial destabilisation is potentially vulnerable in terms of detail. It is quite possible markets, central banks, regulators and markets will increasingly perceive how wrong and damaging their policies have been, and they will start to stumble into cures and solutions we haven't foreseen. There is the famous adage: "Americans will always do the right thing, after first exhausting every other possibility." It is certainly not only possible, but probable, they will eventually spot what is going wrong and try to correct it.

"How" is the question! Every day the great financial distortion continues, and normalisation is not pursued the bubble gets bigger. Its gets more difficult and painful to correct.

We are not concerned. The damage has already been done. The plan is so complex it's highly unlikely that tweaking broken markets to restore one aspect, for instance the level of interest rates, will trigger balance across the whole. In fact, it's more likely that correcting one part will simply cause greater imbalance elsewhere.

The whole financial construct is inherently unstable, and it's looking inconceivable it can be retuned and rebalanced without a Global Financial Reset – the financial equivalent of the Ark – being pressed. Our approach to risk mitigation is simple on The Fifth Horseman Project: Let it Be. Let them try and fix it while we continue to destabilise it.

They won't.
They can't.

Their problem is time is increasingly limited. If rates continue to fall into negative yield territory then no-one is ever going to receive their pensions, or a return on savings which will undermine society as assuredly as anything. This will be made more complex and unruly by rising income inequality and social injustice.

The global central banks are running out of time. They need to choose between a relative short-term global crash and a loss of face for the mistakes of the past 10 years, or they can hang on for a global revolution and financial system reset that will destroy them completely.

Yours

TJ Wormwood

Project Fifth Horseman – L3R7C

CHAIN 13:

Let me see if I can sum this up

From: thedevil@hell.hel

To: tjwormwood@7circle.com

Subject: 5ᵗH - Let me see if I can sum this up

TJ – how does this sound for the Demonic Advisory Board?

"

Uncertainty and Instability are wonderful things. Especially in financial markets. We're confident that the distortions we've created in financial asset prices are leading markets towards an impossible choice between distortion for ever (or at least until no one receives their pension), or an enormous bursting bubble crescendo of crashing hopes and dreams.

It will occur simultaneously across multiple asset classes – equities, credit and government bonds, commodities and funds - when investors finally perceive just how distorted relative to the real-world economy financial assets have become. It will hit every asset class. Few investors will be able to exit – trapped in illiquid securities as the scale of the distortion catastrophe becomes apparent.

A massive collapse in financial asset values will trigger doom and gloom across the global economy triggering a host of secondary effects including deeper protectionism, fear, and hostility.

Alongside the Financial Asset Meltdown, we're engineering a global crisis in money by encouraging MMT, Crypto and companies such as Facebook to reinvent money, and diminish confidence in Government Fiat Money. MMT should prove another vector of contagion into fiat money – triggering impossible demands and expectation that will fuel inflation. Eventually we expect a reversion to almost barter levels of exchange inefficiency.

Flawed political responses and an inability to successful generate solution to ongoing financial crisis will characterise the coming years. Confidence in government and leadership will continue to fall in the line with their failure to lead solutions. Governments will remain distracted from solving pressing social and environmental challenges. Nation states will fracture, split and become less and less relevant.

In short – JOB DONE

Lucifer, Lord of Infinite Darkness

———————————————————————————————

From: TJ Wormwood, L3R7C

To: Lucifer, Lord of Infinite Darkness:

Subject: Re: 5ᵗH - Let me see if I can sum this up

B'LOID

Yes, I think that should tick the boxes...

However, another thought has crossed my mind... Perhaps, there is another, better way to play this.

Rather than simply observing how financial markets bring down mankind, maybe we could participate. We could do so in a proactive way, in a format *Hemself* can't possibly object to? It strikes me our operation on the surface is quite expensive, and this approach would not only cover that, but give us even more options.

May I ask Beelzebub to schedule a meeting at your earliest convenience?

Warmest Regards

TJ Wormwood

Lord 3ʳᵈ Ring, 7ᵗʰ Circle of Hell

POSTSCRIPT:

Pale Horseman Asset Management

From: the.devil@hell.org

To: tjwormwood@7circle.com

Subject: PHAM

TJ

Great Job! Like it. Keep up the pressure.

I think the new plan is even better than Fifth Horseman. As you say, markets always over-estimate the downside and ignore how resilient mankind can be.

I've been checking with the other departments and they think its likely mankind will solve climate change, global warming and all the other challenges, and, despite our very best efforts, *Hemself* will ensure they thrive whatever we do.

That's a good thing because it keeps us in business!

Let's launch the Pale Horseman Asset Management plan. Remember, our goal is unhappiness, not the complete and utter destruction of humanity. Who are we going to torment if you kill them all?

Let's see how it develops and where it takes you.

Keep me informed. We should have a further chat soon. Drop in any time.

NICK

NB – Terrible NY car crash. Sending you tragically deceased bankers for your organ project.

From: TJ Wormwood, L3R7C

To: Lucifer, Lord of Infinite Darkness:

Subject: Re: PHAM

Dear L'LIOD

Thanks for your confidence in the project. We've now set up and launched PALE HORSEMAN ASSET MANAGEMENT, or PHAM as the world knows it.

As we've engineered global financial meltdown, we're in the best place to actively invest and profit from it. If this initiative is successful, then it will be the ultimate insider trade!

Some journalist asked me why I was naming the new fund PHAM – I told them I'd named it after my favourite Sushi restaurant in London. If they ever work it out, we'll just dismiss them as cranky conspiracy theorists.

Here are some of the clippings:

Press Release: PHAM LLC is set to be largest new Hedge Fund launch this year. Set up and led by star investment banker, TJ Wormwood, the fund will follow an Unconstrained Investment Policy.

CIO Thad Wormwood said:

> *"Despite ongoing geopolitical uncertainty, the ongoing distortion in Financial Asset Prices, and the repression of the investment industry through Government, central banks and regulatory policy, PHAM's mission is to focus on Ethical and Environmentally sound investments, with the highest corporate governance standards.*
>
> *PHAM is not about greed and we will labour to undo the per-*

ception finance has driven income inequality. This will be the first hedge fund were the prime rule is that no one can earn more than 10 times the lowest salary. All our profits will be ploughed back into our investments. There will be no cash or stock bonuses. We believe these principles, together with our solid grounding and understanding of markets, due diligence and risk management, will secure our investors fair and above market returns."

I reckon we will have closed most hedge funds within a year or so....

I thought you might like this cutting from Bloomberg:

"In a wide-ranging interview with Bloomberg, Investment hot-shot Thad Wormwood, the principal and CIO of PHAM, repeated his commitment to investment transparency, and said the firm is investing in the expectation of a long-term trade war with China and a correction of current financial asset distortions. The firm's investments in liquid markets include the short end of the US Treasury and German Bund markets, Gold, and a big position in UK government gilts.

When asked if that was unduly defensive, he agreed; *"I wish we could go back to free trade, but political stupidity means we live in very uncertain times, and you have to invest accordingly."* He added the fund considers the UK fundamentally under-valued: *"Everyone assumes the worst – which never happens. The UK will do well after its messy Brexit, and our investment is a rising sterling bet even as the global economy stalls"*, said Wormwood.

While PHAM has gone bearish for the short term, the fund's alternative investments in private equity, pioneer and venture capital look extremely bullish long-term plays. Woodward said: *"We're not buying the mature or struggling tech unicorns – they are bubbles and vulnerable to rising competition. We're looking for the next but one wave of tech invention, so we are investing in Robotics, Artificial Intelligence and especially*

Educational initiatives. We're funding new schools and will innovate new techniques like Virtual Classroom learning, but especially training more and better teachers – sometimes old school is best school."

Asked how PHAM can justify generate revenues from private education, which seems to violate all its equality principals, Wormwood said: *"We don't expect to generate any revenues from our education businesses. Once government realise the value we've created, we hope they acknowledge the value of what we've created and pay us what they cost us to set them up and not a cent more.* [Shortly after this interview, California and Washington state announced they are passing over parts of their education programme to PHAM.] *No student will ever pay a dime for the education we're pioneering. If these costs break our fund, then we will have broken for our honest beliefs. Our return will come from being able to employ the students we educate in high paying roles in the new businesses we are setting up across the economy."*

He went on to add: *"We need trained and motivated engineers to run automated factories and develop our clean renewable energy businesses. We need socially aware bankers and financiers using AI to make sure our clients are getting the best and fairest financial services. We need scientists to fix our environment and clean the oceans and atmosphere. We need expert geneticists and up-skilled farmers using robotics and AI to boost healthy food production. We need more doctors, nurses and care professionals to nurture our society form cradle to grave, and we need technicians to utilise systems and information to do so efficiently."*

Wormwood added: *"Our ambition to make the countries we operate in the most exciting economies on earth. We want everyone to be given the opportunity to participate in it with a proper, well paid and fulfilling job. If people don't want to work, that's their call – and will still provide them with a level of comfort and support that means they don't fall through the cracks. When people are tired and need a long-term break, our new economy will care for them, and deliver them back refreshed. The days of wage slavery and existing just for the job will be ended. We are going to ensure not a single person ever worries again about being able to retire with financial security. And we will do it through Free Markets!"*

Wormwood admits it may take years for his vision to be achieved. When asked if he will respond to the overtures he's been receiving from both political parties in the US; *"Heck, it's great to be noticed and to hear we're making a difference. Maybe at some point in the future, but not yet. If I can make this work, then I'd sure like to give it a shot."*

Wormwood was equally voluble about the investors who've funded PHAM. *"Its no secret we turned down a massive investment from the Church. We felt it would be dishonest to accept money from an organisation that hasn't yet come to terms with the manner in which senior leaders abused people for centuries. Perhaps sometime in the future we can review that decision."*

The speed at which PHAM was able to pull investors into the fund surprised many observers: *"Well after years of investment banking I had a pretty thick address book",* said Wormwood: *"and many of the early investors were personal friends. I might have threatened a few with eternal damnation (laughing) if they didn't invest, but they did... they did..."*

From: the.devil@hell.org

To: tjwormwood@7circle.com

Subject: PHAM

Tad

Like it. Very nice. How is the tuning on your organ? Have you tortured the bishop to middle C yet?

Take this project as far as you can...

Let's schedule a review of the portfolio when you are down here next...

NICK

The END of the Beginning

Printed in Great
Britain
by Amazon